SOUTHERN ENGLAND

First published in Great Britain in 2010 by
Young Writers, Remus House, Coltsfoot Drive,
Peterborough, PE2 9JX
Tel (01733) 890066 Fax (01733) 313524
Website: www.youngwriters.co.uk

Foreword

Since Young Writers was established in 1990, our aim has been to promote and encourage written creativity amongst children and young adults. By giving aspiring young authors the chance to be published, Young Writers effectively nurtures the creative talents of the next generation, allowing their confidence and writing ability to grow.

With our latest fun competition, *The Adventure Starts Here* ..., primary school children nationwide were given the tricky challenge of writing a story with a beginning, middle and an end in just fifty words.

The diverse and imaginative range of entries made the selection process a difficult but enjoyable task with stories chosen on the basis of style, expression, flair and technical skill. A fascinating glimpse into the imaginations of the future, we hope you will agree that this entertaining collection is one that will amuse and inspire the whole family.

Contents

Streatham & Clapham High School, London

The Pointer School, Blackheath

The Study Preparatory School, London

The Mini Sagas

David's Encounter

David screamed loudly as the shadow of a ghost crossed his bedroom. He was shaking like jelly. He saw it again moving across another wall. He shut his eyes tightly at the exact moment his sister crept back to her room, giggling quietly, holding a torch and an action figure.

Ryan Land (10)

The Little Monkey

A monkey was in a tree with green leaves. One day like every other the monkey swang from tree to tree… *Timber*, the tree fell down! the monkey sobbed, 'I loved that tree!' he cried. The monkey perked up, he sighed, 'There's always more trees,' the monkey stumbled away.

Beth Richards (10)
Ashton Middle School, Dunstable

2

The Scary Christmas Eve

It was Christmas Eve and I crept downstairs, but then I saw a shadow coming through the window. I went to the window to see what it was, it could have been a mouth dripping, bloodthirsty, monster but then it came through the window and became fat Santa!

Daniel Fitt (10)

Ashton Middle School, Dunstable

Lost

One day, when Sasha was walking from school she heard a growling noise from the forest. She quietly went to see what it was. When she got there, she saw a figure and she was sure what it was. It was a monster!
'Boo!' shouted Kate, Sasha's best friend.

Alanna Smart (9)
Ashton Middle School, Dunstable

Pirate Attack

There I was on the Seven seas with Blue Beard
Boyak. He approached me with his deadly sword
and gold gun. *Bang!* He shot. Although it wasn't
him who shot. It was my amazing dad! The ugly
pirates were angry.
'Surprise,' it was the best birthday present
surprise ever!

George Kemp (10)
Ashton Middle School, Dunstable

Monster

In the afternoon she went outside and there stood the horrible, ugly, deadly creature. The girl said, 'Please don't hurt me, I'm only ten, I'm very innocent! Here look, you can eat my sweet if you want to!'
Then the creature laughed and said, 'Don't be silly, it's me, Amber.'

Paige Mitchell (9)
Ashton Middle School, Dunstable

6

The Cheese Ball!

Amy was watching TV when she heard a rustle coming from the kitchen. She went into the kitchen but there was nothing there except a bag of cheese balls! She turned back round, it rustled again so she opened the packet. There was only one there. 'Weird!' She said confused.

Harlee Judge (10)
Ashton Middle School, Dunstable

The Battle Against The Dead Zombies

It was Monday morning at 8am. *Ding, ding, ding.*
'Oh no, I'm late for school!' shouted Callum
madly.
'Hello! Hello! Mum, Dad, where are you? Help!
It's the dead Zombies, they're after me. Huh? Oh
it's just the mailman! What are you doing at this
time?' asked Callum softly.

Callum Kerwick (10)
Ashton Middle School, Dunstable

8

The Sweet Shop

Maisie walked into the sweet shop. It was dark
and she was very scared. She stood in the middle
of the shop. She heard a noise, but it was just
a bird that hit the glass window. She walked
towards the counter and stopped. Then the
shopkeeper jumped up! *Ahhh!*

Eleanor Abel (10)
Ashton Middle School, Dunstable

The Edge Of The Earth

A man was walking on the edge of the Earth. He was thinking, when suddenly a creature with fangs appeared before his eyes. He started to run, but where could he go? He ran towards a river, it was the only place to go. Luckily, it was only a dream!

Jessica Smith (10)

Ashton Middle School, Dunstable

Untitled

In the hot, steaming forest a man was on a mission to kill the Amazonian dragon. It swooped down, he ducked and closed his eyes tightly. When he looked at the dragon it was on his back, rolling about like a dog. They were best friends forever and ever.

Darrell Njogu (10)
Ashton Middle School, Dunstable

The Scary Hotdog Man

There was a sausage and two sauces. A boy called Toby was walking and saw a thing in the distance, booming at him saying, 'I will chop you up and eat you, eat you!'
It was then, Toby realised that it was just a silly old hotdog man screaming.

Melissa Southern (10)
Ashton Middle School, Dunstable

Scared!

One cold, dark, wet afternoon. A cold girl stepped into her house. She looked around but nothing and nobody was there. What had happened? Where was all the furniture? Then she suddenly heard a bang from upstairs! Someone jumped out at her. It was only her parents, they were redecorating.

Jennifer Darling (10)
Ashton Middle School, Dunstable

13

A Deserted House

When Beth got home the house was deserted!
The chairs were broken, windows were cracked!
There was a horrific squeak from the door, a
wrinkled hand came from inside the door, then a
wrinkled face with round glasses. Beth trembled
with fear.
'I'm home!' someone shouted loudly.
'Oh, hi Nan!'

Leah Thompson (10)
Ashton Middle School, Dunstable

14

The Prank

Kirsty walked into the woods. She thought there were more trees. Something made a bang, it was a bear.
'Help!' she screamed in horror. The bear started to charge at her. The bear opened its mouth. She kept running. Then suddenly realised that she was on a prank TV show.

Katy Kemp (9)
Ashton Middle School, Dunstable

Little Big Adventure

I was walking home but when I arrived the house
was empty. I looked around but nobody was
home then a man emerged from the shadows and
turned the light on.
'Hello Grandson!'
'Oh, ur hi.'
'Surprise!' bellowed everyone.
'Wow!' what a great birthday party!
'Thanks so much Mum!'

Samuel Shooter (10)
Ashton Middle School, Dunstable

All Locked Up

As he walked into the metal door he heard loads
of loud footsteps. Joe started to panic in his prison
cell. As the shadow of the creature grew and
grew Joe's heart pounded until he could feel his
heart hit his chest. The creature shouted, 'Here's
your food, you criminal!'

Reece Lock (10)
Ashton Middle School, Dunstable

17

The Surprise next Door

Sophie ran up to her new next door neighbour's door and knocked. Then the door opened. The house was full of cobwebs but no one in sight. 'Hello?' she shouted. Then suddenly out of nowhere a man covered in blood said, 'I'm Simon, could you help me redecorate please?'

Grace Fitzsimmons (9)

Ashton Middle School, Dunstable

The Horrifying Witch

I woke up one day ready to go to school, as I yawned and opened my eyes, there was a monster with a warty face, rotten black teeth, grey hair and a horrifying big boil on her face. 'Say hello to your Grandma!' said Mum. *Phew!* it was only Grandma.

Nikhil Mathews Jiji (10)
Ashton Middle School, Dunstable

Trip To America

David Jones went on a flight to America to see his friends and family. When he got there he couldn't quite find them. He thought he was lost! Then he suddenly heard two voices up ahead calling his name. He walked forward and saw his whole family and his friends.

Rhianne Penn (10)
Ashton Middle School, Dunstable

Nothing Scary About The Ice Cream Lady

My house was the next road, I didn't think anyone
was at home. I saw a scary person approaching
me, blood on hands!
'Hello, it's the ice cream lady,' said Sarah.
'Oh, is that blood?' Abby replied.
'Strawberry sauce!' she replied',
'Want an ice cream?' Said Sarah.
'No,' Abby replied.

Regan Madden (10)
Ashton Middle School, Dunstable

The Sauce Seller

It was evening, David went down the alley to buy some sauce. He went into the shop, he wasn't alone in the shop. The sauce was £2, he only had £1, he went. On his way back he saw a man covered in blood.

'Selling sauce,' said the sauce seller.

Wojciech Demucha (10)
Ashton Middle School, Dunstable

Untitled

I came home with a loaf of bread, knocked on
the door waiting for an answer, I knocked again,
still nothing. I pulled on the handle, it was open! I
walked in,
'Mum, Dad?' there was nothing. I was uneasy.
Then out of nowhere,
'Trick or treat?'
It was Halloween.

Isabella Bedlington (10)
Ashton Middle School, Dunstable

Midnight Surprise

It was a cold, dark night. Zoe slowly walked herself home from a terrific day at school. Zoe held onto the knob tightly and twisted it. She turned and pushed it open. Her heart thumped, the lights flickered and... *bang!*
'Surprise! Happy birthday sweetheart, do you like it?'

Hannah Smith (11)
Ashton Middle School, Dunstable

24

Champions Or Losers

It was 2-2 with one minute to go, Nathan ran. He stepped past the defenders with his skill, only the goalie to beat. I could score from here, my nan could score from here, he's only gone and… I heard a roar. We won! Champions of the world! 'Hooray! Hooray!'

Nathan Davies (11)
Ashton Middle School, Dunstable

Goal!

It is all up to Gerrard; if he scores we win, if he misses we lose.
Like a bullet he hits the top corner, the goalie dives the right way. Does he save it or not? I hear a cheer… England have won, Gerrard scored! I can't believe it! *Woopedeedoo!*

Hayden Duffy-Flitton (11)
Ashton Middle School, Dunstable

Haunted House

I was in the house and nobody was there. I heard a creak, then suddenly the door banged open. A man jumped into the room, we screamed so loud the house shook. We ran into the next room but he was following us. He took his mask off, it's Dad!

Nathan Prescott (11)

Ashton Middle School, Dunstable

The Intruder!

Bob entered his house. All the lights were off. He started to feel uneasy. The door creaked open, he peered in. There was a pale figure, it went upstairs, Bob went upstairs. 'Boo!'
He thought he was going to die. It took its cloak off.
Ahhh! it was silly Dad.

Alexander Tagg (10)

Ashton Middle School, Dunstable

The Haunted Graveyard

I was walking happily through the graveyard, I hear a crack, a skeleton flung from its grave. It roared and chased us down the road. We ran into someone's garden. The skeleton followed close by. The sun was coming up, the sun came up fully. The skeleton turned to dust.

Michael Button (10)
Ashton Middle School, Dunstable

The Scary Cake

When I closed the door, I heard a loud bang from the kitchen. I went in and there was a terrifying, scary piece of cake. It was juicy and it wanted to eat me. I screamed but all the cake did was show his scary, sharp, terrifying fangs to me.

Joe Church (11)

Ashton Middle School, Dunstable

Ham

Once upon a time there was a girl called Lucy who loved ham. She said to her Mum. 'Can I have some ham?'
She said no but Lucy went to the fridge and took some ham and ate all of it. She was eating it under the table, naughty Lucy!

Lucy Fairclough (11)
Ashton Middle School, Dunstable

Cheese!

Once there was a girl who loved cheese.
Especially melted cheddar, *yum…*
She asked her mum if she could go to the shop to
get some cheese. Her mum said, 'Go on get some
cheese for £2.50.' She went from her house to
the shop but they ran out. *Grrr…*

Emily Betts (10)
Ashton Middle School, Dunstable

The Dark House

There was a dark house, on a dark hill, in a dark
forest. In the dark house, there was a room,
in the room there was a box, in the box there
was…
Bang! The closet door opened. Cautiously I
walked in… There it was - my teddy! 'I lost that!'

Freya Surman (10)
Ashton Middle School, Dunstable

Lost In The Desert

Lost in the desert. Arms are heavy, he is very confused. Scared of death, he fights to survive. Scrambling to get food he's fussy. He can't find anything he would like to eat. He doesn't make it. Oh well, besides, he is a penguin. I don't really like penguins anyway.

Saavan Chavda (11)

Ashton Middle School, Dunstable

The Knight

The knight set off on his quest to kill the dragon.
He rode on his horse till he reached the cave. He
went in the cave to find the dragon sleeping. So
he killed the dragon and the land was safe again.
The knight was rewarded with some money.

Freddie Thornton (11)

Ashton Middle School, Dunstable

The Inspector

18th March 1998, 'Today inspector Janet is
coming to look at the hotel!' said agent 0740.
ding, dong, went the door bell,
'I bet that's her.' Agent 0740 said anxiously. I
opened the door slowly.
'Hello, agent 0740.' Said inspector Janet, poshly.
She stepped in.
'Very clean.' She said.
'What's happening?'

Ellen Cox (10)

Ashton Middle School, Dunstable

36

Hunger Or Death

A black shadow lurked in the red sea… it was
my pet, a great white shark, his name is Bitey. He
opened his mouth for me to put some fish in. I
screamed very loud.
'Yum!' Cried the killer whale. 'He was very nice
to eat. Yum, yum, yum!'

James Palmer (11)
Ashton Middle School, Dunstable

The Horror Of Mum's

I sat there alone. *What a surprise,* I thought, *no one is home.* Then I heard a creek, footsteps approached me. I looked around. Nothing! A shadow appeared on the ground, it started growing. Suddenly everything went cold. It felt like someone walked over my grave.
'It's me!' Only Mum.

Lara-Skye Haigh (10)
Ashton Middle School, Dunstable

Halloween Horror

The man waddled into the room. The lights
flickered on and off as he went to grab the handle
and open the door. He slowly opened the banging
door. No one was there. As he sat down, the
door banged again. He opened the door. It was a
vampire. 'Boo!'
Argh!

Tyler-James Clark (11)
Ashton Middle School, Dunstable

39

Bob And The Cake

As Bob walked into his own house he heard a
smash. It was more quiet than usual. Suddenly the
lights flickered on.
'Surprise!'
He had been thrown a surprise party. They
passed Bob his cake. He blew out the candles.
'Argh!'
A gorilla attacked Bob and ate him all up.

Owen Borrett (11)
Ashton Middle School, Dunstable

Fox And Rabbit

Slowly, the rabbit poked its head out of the rabbit
hole. It was safe so she crept out. Close by, a fox
lurked ready to pounce. Suddenly, the fox started
chasing the rabbit.
'Help! Help!' Squeaked the rabbit. They ran and
ran and the fox fell down a hole. *Hooray!*

Abigail Peacham (10)
Ashton Middle School, Dunstable

41

Surprise Welcome Back

Lauren was walking down the dark street. It was deserted, there was nobody around. It was getting late and Lauren needed to go home. As she was walking home, she saw shadows lurking. She ran home, her heart pounding. When she got there she saw everyone.
'Welcome back,' they said.

Charlotte Lane (11)
Ashton Middle School, Dunstable

42

Scary Screaming Halloween

It was Halloween! A girl went trick or treating.
She went to an abandoned house. The door was
wide open so she went in. She heard creaks, but
before anything, she was trapped. She couldn't
escape… then she woke up. 'It's a dream. I can
go back to sleep now!'

Maisie Spokes (10)
Ashton Middle School, Dunstable

The Spooky Shadow!

Susan was strolling home after school. She was
excited to see the snow. Suddenly she could
hear crunching behind her... after that shadows
started to appear! Susan was frightened so she
ran but the shadow wouldn't leave her alone! She
opened her door. Then she noticed it was her
shadow!

Chloe Dunn (10)

Ashton Middle School, Dunstable

No Noise, No Go

One morning I woke up and there was no movement, no rustling of paper from Dad, no kettle boiling from Mum. Not even an annoying little sister bugging me. I went into the cupboard and all three of them were tied up. I wondered what had happened.

Kieran O'Neill (10)

Ashton Middle School, Dunstable

45

Bang!

Bang! Bang! Nathan covered his head… *Bang! Bang!*
What's going on? He thought as he started to crawl home. *Bang! Bang!* He picked up his pace and was at the front door of his house, where he discovered bullet holes in the front door.

George Carter (10)
Ashton Middle School, Dunstable

The Curse Of The Micker

Once upon a time there was a boy called Rick.
He went through the park one evening and he
saw a Micker. It was walking towards him slowly.
It was slodgy and rubbery and then… Rick
slowly walked backwards and he slammed into a
tombstone and he was knocked unconscious.

Ryan Luff (10)
Ashton Middle School, Dunstable

47

Spider In The Cellar

Amy walked in to the cellar. It was very dark and scary. She slowly went down the steps. Suddenly, she heard something.

What was that? she thought. A giant spider came into view.

'Argh!' she cried and she went to tell someone quickly.

Karis Watling (10)
Ashton Middle School, Dunstable

The Disappearing People

Jess went to the park where she was going to meet her friends. When she got there the park was empty. Nobody to be seen. There was a weird sound of silence, it was never silent. Where was everybody? There was a rustling sound behind her. What was it?

Marie Want (9)

Ashton Middle School, Dunstable

The Fright In The Night

One day there lived a fat cat called Pat. Pat was very cheeky, Pat went out one night to a party with the other cats. When the party was over he went home, tired and achy. Pat got home, the lights were off and suddenly, *Boo!* Pat died of fright.

Benjamin Sharp (10)
Ashton Middle School, Dunstable

The Spooks

One day there lived a boy called Jack. He went in the woods at night. He saw some shadows in the distance and jumped! He carried on walking and found the shadows were his mum and dad. He was so relieved.

Danielle Stewart (10)

Ashton Middle School, Dunstable

Anna's Birthday

'Happy birthday Anna,' cried her mum and dad
happily.
'Why don't you make a wish?' asked Anna's dad
cheerfully.
'OK!' Anna closed her eyes and made her wish,
but when she opened her eyes Mum and Dad had
gone and the lights were off.
'Hello?' whispered Anna. But nobody answered.

Lydia Banton (10)
Ashton Middle School, Dunstable

52

Ghost Town

The officer was walking in the dark ghost town
taking cover behind every wall in sight. Then he
saw the enemy so he got out his gun and shot
them. He missed so they both ran but luckily he
found a shotgun and shot the enemy.

Jack Pendle (9)
Ashton Middle School, Dunstable

What A Scare

Lucy entered the bedroom tiredly. Suddenly she heard footsteps in the playroom. She went in the playroom. She walked to one of the cupboards and flung the cupboard doors open! It had nothing except her toys. She opened the next cupboard. It was her dog. What a scare.

Jamie Dixon (10)
Ashton Middle School, Dunstable

The Tabby Cat And The Lonely Cat

A small tabby cat was wandering through the park. She met a lonely cat. 'Hello,' she whispered. 'Hi,' he replied. They went on a stroll together and found some fish, so they shared it. The tabby forgot to go home so she rushed home, but never forgot that wonderful day.

Maya Thanky (10)
Ashton Middle School, Dunstable

The Playful Dog

As Lily quietly walked into the silent room she started to whistle and her dog, Lightning, came running in with a ball. 'Hello boy,' said Lily stroking him. 'Come on, let's go outside.' 'Oh no, I've lost the ball!' sobbed Lily. 'Lightning, you're not supposed to bury it!' she laughed.

Lauren Hildreth (10)

Ashton Middle School, Dunstable

The Creepy School

Hannah arrived at school. It was deserted but the door was unlocked. She walked in slowly. It was messy and the lockers were gone. She went home. Then she remembered the letter in her bag. It said they were decorating the school and the pupils had a day off.

Charlotte Jackson (10)
Ashton Middle School, Dunstable

Dreams

I was trapped in the corner of a cave with two robbers closing in on me, one with a gun. The guy with the gun shot it, it missed me by an inch. Suddenly I woke up in a hot sweat, was it all just a bad dream?

Kira McMinn-Loughlin (9)
Ashton Middle School, Dunstable

Thirst For Trouble

Sarah crept out of her room in the house, there
was a crashing noise! She tiptoed downstairs to
find it was just Mum who'd dropped a glass of
water. 'Oops!' Mum said after.
'I was getting you a drink for bed!'
Oh well. At least I am not thirsty now!

Natasha Brown (10)
Ashton Middle School, Dunstable

My Dad

My dad got up as usual for work at 6am. When he arrived at work he unlocked all the doors but as he unlocked the door his key snapped off. 'Oh no!' he shouted, so he rang the locksmith who came very quickly and he changed the locks.

Andi Taylor (9)
Ashton Middle School, Dunstable

The Haunted House!

One night a house stood in the distance all alone in the dark. The lights were flickering on and off. Something jumped behind me. I rang the doorbell. The door creaked opened. There was a record playing crackling music. It was freaky but in the end it was a friend.

Sasha Fenwick (10)
Ashton Middle School, Dunstable

The Evil Girl

Once there was an evil girl who lived in a dark and damp house with no one to play with. Then a new girl came to her house. She knocked, no one answered. She still went in because the door was open, but till now we've never seen her again.

Emily Mollison (10)
Ashton Middle School, Dunstable

Golden Ship

The Golden Ship reached the dock.
'That's weird!' Thought the captain,
'People are usually waiting eagerly to jump aboard
this party ship.' The captain peered into the
darkness when suddenly a crowd of people with
party poppers appeared.
'Surprise! Happy 10th birthday Golden Ship!'
'Wow!' said captain, 'Jump aboard!'

Liam Smith (10)
Ashton Middle School, Dunstable

The Dark And Stormy Surprise

It was a dark and stormy night. Francesca was stuck in her room and the power had just gone out. She heard noises downstairs and so many voices. She began to feel very scared.
A few hours later, *bang!* Her door opened and she ran downstairs to a party.

Kyrie Day (10)
Ashton Middle School, Dunstable

64

The Cellars Death

A cleaner in the school went down to the cellar for a mop. She heard a noise and saw a flash of a blade! The next thing she knew she was waking up next to a body, it was the head teacher! He was not dead, he was still breathing.

Miles Capp (9)
Ashton Middle School, Dunstable

Scary Shadows

One weird and strange day Josh was walking
home with his friend, he turned around and he
wasn't there.
'Where are you? Are you OK?' Josh kept on
walking and he saw a very scary shadow. Slowly
he had a look … it was his friend, they both
laughed.
'Ha, ha.'

Joshua McGhee (10)
Ashton Middle School, Dunstable

The Haunted Mansion

One day an old mansion stood above the town.
This mansion was haunted by a ghost. One day a
man went in and died, his name was Bob. It was a
cold day he got dared to go in and died.

Ewan Matthews (10)
Ashton Middle School, Dunstable

Home Alone

It was a dark and stormy night and I was left at home all alone, on my birthday. When I spoke I heard an echo. I was trying to get to sleep but all I could hear was the sound of the owls hooting in my ears.

Chloe Gray (10)

Ashton Middle School, Dunstable

A Dark And Cold Night

It was a dark, cold night, the owls were hooting.
I was scared. Mum popped to the shops and Dad
was at work. Then all of a sudden there was a
banging coming up to my room. I was so scared
but it was only my mum, I was OK then!

Nathan Holden (10)

Ashton Middle School, Dunstable

Haunted Mansion

One dark, gloomy night a young girl called Julia walked into a haunted mansion. Julia knocked on the door but no one opened. She turned her back then someone opened it. She went in! A few days later, all that was left of her was a pile of her bones.

Charlotte Pryor (10)
Ashton Middle School, Dunstable

Camping Gone Wrong

'Yes,' Bob screamed loudly. He started dancing
and screaming,
'We're going camping.'
So at 8pm they got everything ready and they ran
out in the hail, rain, thunder and lightning. They
didn't care about the weather… By 6am they had
changed their minds because their tent had been
blown away.

Oliver Dee (9)
Ashton Middle School, Dunstable

Friends

The garden gate swung open as she approached
it. The wind bellowed. Sarah didn't know what to
do. Her friend had left her. A bright light shone
through the gate. She opened it, worried about
what she was going to come across.
'Hello!' she called.
'Surprise!' her friends shouted loudly.

Abigail Marshall (12)
Ashton Middle School, Dunstable

Haunted House

The door creaked open, so I stepped inside. I paused, the wind blew the door shut behind me. *Bang!* I tiptoed forward carefully, slowly. *Am I alone?* I thought to myself. I peered round the corner into the dull, lifeless kitchen. Is there a monster in this abandoned, old house?

Charlotte Tubb (12)
Ashton Middle School, Dunstable

The Monster From Under The Bed

She tiptoed up the never-ending stairway waiting for disaster to strike. It did. The monster from under the bed pounced! She rushed to the window, screaming for help. None came. She dived for the light switch. Silence! The monster disappeared back into the dark shadows...
Lurking!

Flora Dempsey (12)
Ashton Middle School, Dunstable

Home Alone

Home alone. A creaking on the stairs, my
breathing quickened. I flicked on the light.
Another creak. Checking the stairs, I felt hot
breath on my neck. I turned, screaming, kicking
out with my legs.
'Ow!' She screamed, 'What are you doing?'
'Oh, it's you, Mum!' I sighed with relief.

Emma Doggett (12)
Ashton Middle School, Dunstable

Rapunzel Visits The Seven Dwarves' Home

'Hi ho, hi ho, it's off to work we go. A skip, skip
here and a snip, snip there. Hi ho, hi ho.'
'What'll it be today Rapunzel?'
'Three on the top and four on the sides.'
Snip, snip.
'All done, here's a mirror.'
'Oooh … I'm bald!'
'Tee-hee. Tee-hee!'

Bradley Coan (11)
Ashton Middle School, Dunstable

The Forest Lights

Alone in the fearsome forest. Looked left, looked right, there was no way out. Then a light came from straight ahead, I started walking in hope for a sign! However as I approached it was just a small white torch floating in mid-air... Slowly backing away, I screamed, 'Ghost!'

Megan Saunders (12)
Ashton Middle School, Dunstable

The School Hallway

Alone, Silent, Deserted. Was there anywhere to
go? Was the ceiling falling in or were the windows
getting closer? It was the end of second lesson.
In the blink of an eye Katie had fainted, she was
traumatised, petrified. Children gathered around
the body, looking worried. It was a nightmare.

Phoebe Howard (11)

Ashton Middle School, Dunstable

The Haunted Mansion

I'm creeping through the abandoned mansion.
It'll be mine when I'm older. I'm dreading it. I'm
hopping up the stairs. There's a crash from the
bedroom. I wander in. It's empty apart from a
bed and a wardrobe. I pull back the moth-eaten
covers. Something jumps from the wardrobe …

Hannah Charters (11)
Ashton Middle School, Dunstable

Frightening But Funny!

I opened the shattered door. I walked across the creaky floorboards.

'Hello?' I whispered. 'I know you're here.' My heart racing, legs like jelly, I walked into the room, the black, frightening room … Someone grabbed me. The lights flicked on, *Argh!*

'You scared me!' I mumbled as I started laughing.

Rebecca Ruffles (12)
Ashton Middle School, Dunstable

What Is It?

Footsteps pattered on the kitchen floor in the
night. He got up armed with a water gun, scared
of what he would find. He tiptoed down the
stairs to the big, oak kitchen door, pots and pans
crashing to the floor, he turned the handle…
Miaow! It's the cat!

Daniel Grantham (12)
Ashton Middle School, Dunstable

The Shadow

The lights were off. The house ached. Time stood still. The sound of my heart was the only noise. *Thump, thump.* Suddenly I wasn't alone. *Who was it?* I thought. Something fluttered by my cheek ... the wind? Moonlight illuminated the dusty floor. A shadow appeared in front of me ...

Natasha Soper (12)

Ashton Middle School, Dunstable

The Deserted Street

She was alone, walking down the deserted street,
only light from one flickering lamp post. She could
hear the sound of breathing behind her but didn't
dare to turn. It came closer and closer, she could
feel the breathing on her neck, then …
'Stop! I don't like scary ghost stories!'

Rebecca Kemp (11)
Ashton Middle School, Dunstable

The Race

She was running and running, she was nearly at
the finish line. *Yeah!* She sped past the line, then
all of the other athletes ran ahead of her. While
Jess was jumping with joy, people shouted, '*Go!*'
Jess was confused… then she remembered she
had another lap. '*Oh man!*'

Aimee Lau (11)

Ashton Middle School, Dunstable

The Park

The metal park gate swung open, Sarah walked in. Birds fluttered around her as swings swung in the breeze. She knew this way was quicker but something made her unsure of it. Dogs barked in the distance, clouds turned grey and thunder shook the ground. Sarah was never seen again.

Alexandra Farnfield (12)
Ashton Middle School, Dunstable

The Silhouette

Sophie was afraid, she was alone. She wept and cried, calling for help. Finally, moonlight shone. She saw a silhouette run past, now she was scared, not knowing what to do. She saw the silhouette once again, she looked around … Nothing. Something pushed her down. 'Night, night,' whispered a dark silhouette.

Jamaal Jackson (11)
Ashton Middle School, Dunstable

Shadow

Vanessa sneaked quietly into the dark room.
She rushed through the mirrored hallway,
sneaked into the great hall, then swarmed into
the grand bedroom. She bared her teeth, her
fangs glistening with red liquid. A dark silhouette
projected dimly on the wall. There was a scream.
The shadow's arm dropped.

Ellie Broadstock (12)
Ashton Middle School, Dunstable

Thump! Thump! Thump!

There was a noise, *thump! Thump! Thump!*
Coming from downstairs, bags rustled, bells rang.
Thump!
Jessica went downstairs with a gun to see what it
was. Breathing heavily she carefully and cautiously
walked.
Thump! Thump!
She opened the squeaky door. *Eeeekkk!*
'Ho, ho, ho!' It's Father Christmas!

Janiece Jackson (11)
Ashton Middle School, Dunstable

Downstairs In My Night Dress

Down the creaky staircase I am forced to go.
Creak, creak what's that noise? Slowly I walked
in my nightdress. Slowly I turn around with fear.
There it was, the most horrifying sight. An ugly
beast is hunting me with its looks. 'Help, help,
help…'
To be continued …

Eliza Ankra (11)
Ashton Middle School, Dunstable

The Cave Monster

Once there was a girl called Rose. Rose loved to explore. One day she went into a dark cave. She never knew there was a green slimy monster. Suddenly the monster came out of a corner and took her away. She was never seen again.

Kirsty Want (9)
Ashton Middle School, Dunstable

A Crazy Pirate Story

It was a dark and stormy night, I was on a ship only a small cabin to take cover. Lightning struck. How were we staying alive? The magic sphere of the world had a button to stop and start storms so we didn't have a storm like that again.

Mason Keane (10)

Ashton Middle School, Dunstable

At The Park

I was at the park playing football and tennis with
my friends Jimmy, Vern, Roy and Bob. We were
playing football at first. I was drawing 1-1 until I
scored from the half way line. We won 2-1. Next
we played tennis, I won.

Mitchell Butler (10)

Ashton Middle School, Dunstable

The Big Surprise

One day the boy went home and played his Xbox 360, then someone rang the doorbell. He answered but no one was there. He went to the field, his friends jumped out on him. They played football. The boy went home and played his Xbox for four hours.

Lee Frost-Bryant (9)
Ashton Middle School, Dunstable

The Story Of A Ghost Freak

One gusty night, a ghost called Ghostfreak swept over the town. The families below in the town did not notice a young child getting snatched from his bed at midnight. In the morning the little boy's parents looked high and low, but the little boy's life had been claimed.

Lewis Yesinkas (10)
Ashton Middle School, Dunstable

Never Go In The Woods On Your Own!

In the dark woods was a dog who loved eating
people. What Kelly didn't know was he liked to
eat girls with the name Kelly. One day she chased
her dog in the forest. The next day she was
nowhere to be seen. There was only her golden
earring left.

Emily Wadia (10)
Ashton Middle School, Dunstable

Getting Up

I got up and uncoiled my slippery, scaly snake body. Why do mornings have to be such a battle? Today's going to be a big, big day for me. I've got to fight for my dinner, scavenge for water and then get home without getting spotted by a huge giant!

Abby Puddefoot (11)
Ashton Middle School, Dunstable

Chicken Licken

Chicken Licken woke up to a bright and sunny
morning. He dreamed today was going to be
a fantastic day. He flapped his wings, stood up
straight and ran as fast as his little legs could carry
him into the bright, red barn, shouting very, very
loudly.
'Good morning everyone!'

Harrison Cocker (9)
Ashton Middle School, Dunstable

How My Grandad Died

How'd my grandad die you ask? I'll tell you. He fell off a cliff and landed on a ten foot spike. It pierced his colon and he was gone. A week later someone said they saw me at the scene of his death. I had pushed him right off.

Harry Shelley (11)
Ashton Middle School, Dunstable

Where Is The Cup?

It was all down to Gerrard. Like a bullet, he
smashed the ball into the top corner. He was in
ecstasy in front of the crowd. The Liverpool team
went berserk. As the Queen went to present the
trophy, a robber snatched the cup. Worry swept
across their pale faces.

Joseph Field (11)
Ashton Middle School, Dunstable

Hide-And-Go-Seek

One day a mother and child had a game of hide
and go seek. The mum was counting one, two,
three, four, five, six, seven, eight, nine …
The mother was looking everywhere so she rang
his phone number but nobody answered. She
opened the door, he was there. *Woop!*

Wesley Moore (11)
Ashton Middle School, Dunstable

The Mouse Hunter

In Lone town a terrible giant, sharp-clan mouse came to invade. A sharp-clan is a mouse with sharp claws. The mouse hunter gathered his armour and looked for the mouse, no sooner he shouted a battle cry and tied its legs up to a bar. Suddenly it disappeared in mist.

Tyrell Young (10)
Ashton Middle School, Dunstable

The Tea Party

A rabbit went to a chicken's house. The chicken
said, 'Welcome.'
The rabbit replied, 'Thank you.'
The chicken invited the rabbit for tea and the
rabbit said, 'Thank you.' Then the rabbit went
home and had biscuits. After, he went outside to
play on his shiny new swing.

Aruni Kangeyan (9)
Ashton Middle School, Dunstable

Silence

Lucy sat silently outside the headmaster's office.
She shivered thinking she was alone, but suddenly
the lights went out. She hugged herself thinking it
was only a power-cut, but she heard the school
stairs creaking. A woman appeared. Lucy gasped,
but when the woman saw her… She disappeared.

Neave Charlotte Glennon (10)
Ashton Middle School, Dunstable

Magic Marvin

Once upon a time, there lived a magician called
Marvin. He lived in a grey and gloomy castle with
his pet bat, Bert. One day Marvin and Bert went
to a wizard shop. Bert flew off and accidentally
banged into a glass of frog juice. Bert turned into
a frog!

Jade Groom (10)
Ashton Middle School, Dunstable

The Little Girl And The Dog

One day there was a little girl who was ten, she went out to the park to walk her dog, Toby. They both had a great day together. When they were home for dinner they had burgers, then she went into the lounge to watch EastEnders.

Holly Pryor (10)
Ashton Middle School, Dunstable

The Blind Lady

One day a lady called Sophia went to the
supermarket.
'Excuse me, where are the potatoes?' she asked.
'Are you blind? Girls are dumb.' Replied the
shopkeeper!
'Oi, watch your mouth. Show me where the
potatoes are, 'cause I am blind!'

Taylar Charles (10)
Ashton Middle School, Dunstable

Untitled

Kelly walked into the house. She was sure the babysitter was supposed to be there. A sudden creak occurred and there was a walking mummy!

Una Musiwacho
Ashton Middle School, Dunstable

The Intruder

I got home, all I saw was my friend. He was dead.
I heard a smash, I went into the kitchen and
turned on the lights. Then I went into the front
room, there were two shadows. It was scary.
Then they came up to me and killed me! *Argh!*

Neo Yee Keow (10)
Ashton Middle School, Dunstable

The Halloween Crew

Tap! Tap! Tap! Someone was knocking on the door. Harry opened it and was hit by water! He opened his eyes and looked upon the face of ten monsters.
'Hi! We are the Halloween crew!' they said.
'Really?' Harry said.
'And we want some sweets!' they all shouted extremely loudly.

Jamie Hose (9)
Ashton Middle School, Dunstable

The Boy And The Gun

The boy went up to the dreaded table. He
reached out and said, 'No but yes!'
He took the gun, 'I will rule the Universe!'
He shot the gun into the air. Then he ran around
the room, 'Yes, yes, I will!'
The mum walked in, 'Oh deary me, A new bubble
gun!'

Daniel Vines (10)
Ashton Middle School, Dunstable

Poor Jimmy

Poor Jimmy went to school bored and tired and sick of it all. Poor Jimmy had to walk all the way to his classroom. Poor Jimmy walked up the stairs sulking and puffing as he went. Happy Jimmy saw a clown jumping and juggling.

Florence Barshall (8)
Garden House School, London

Ghost

Daniel sat on the sofa. He could hear the ghostly noises. There they were, silhouettes of ghosts dancing on the wall. Smoke was drifting across the room. *It must be a ghost,* thought Daniel. It was all coming from the kitchen then somebody came in ... Mum was Daniel's cooking ghost!

Daniel Moore (10)

Innsworth Junior School, Gloucester

I Have To Write A Story In Fifty Words

I have to write a story in fifty words. I sit down
start pondering, wondering thinking about what
to write. I chew the end off my pencil. Should it
be something scary, exciting sad or funny? Yes! An
idea hit me. I write it down. I've finally finished
my story.

Sarah Dummett (11)
Innsworth Junior School, Gloucester

Big Fright

Once, a girl called Lisa had a dog called Scruff
she had got for her birthday. Suddenly she lost
her dog on a walk. She ran and ran and then she
found him in the local bakery.
'Oh Scruff!' She exclaimed. 'You could have
waited for me! Let's go home.'

Fiona Wilson (11)

Innsworth Junior School, Gloucester

114

The Flickering Light

John was watching TV when suddenly there was a power cut. John rose from his chair and went towards the kitchen. He slowly turned the handle, not knowing what to expect. As the door groaned and creaked the lights flickered back on, Surprise! His family started singing, 'Happy birthday.'

Cameron Levett (9)

Innsworth Junior School, Gloucester

Bullied

My story is about a girl named Polly, she cried until her heart had no tears left. Slowly she got her pillow and put her head inside it. She had never felt so lonely. Guess what had happened, she had been bullied!

Morgan Robinson (10)

Innsworth Junior School, Gloucester

The Fantastical Beast

This gargantuan creature lives in a chthonic
undercity. This extraordinary animal has piercing
horns, flaming eyes, bulging muscles. This
creature is called Verrock. This animal lives to
take over the world. This devious creature is
everywhere and lives at the top of the highest
peak in the entire nation.

Brandon Cox-Fellows (10)
Innsworth Junior School, Gloucester

117

Nightmare

I couldn't sleep. I stared at the cobwebbed
covered window. Suddenly, the rocking horse
moved squeakily. I glanced at my doll, its eyes
stared. My heart thumped. I grabbed my teddy
but that seemed evil. Then something shook my
arm rapidly calling, 'Wake up, or you'll be late for
school.'

Ellie Woodrow (10)
Innsworth Junior School, Gloucester

118

The Chase

Ben was sprinting down an alley. Something was
running after him. Everything went dark. His legs
became tired. He ran behind a house. He was
quickly panting, hoping it wouldn't find him. Then
suddenly a cold hand touched him on the back.
'Tag! You're it!' said Tim. Ben frowned miserably.

Ieuan Boughton (11)
Innsworth Junior School, Gloucester

Untitled

I got home from school.
'Hello, hello, anyone here?' no reply. It was my
birthday, I was at least hoping they were going to
be home. I slowly walked upstairs. My parent's
door was shut, cautiously I opened it, there was a
present, I opened it. *Ohhh!* Nothing there.

Corin Hughes (10)
Innsworth Junior School, Gloucester

Harry Potter And The Boo Of Joy

Harry, Ron, Hermione, Malfoy and Joshua were
looking for the werewolf but Lord Voldemot
jumped out of a bush 'Boo!' said Hagrid.
'Boo!' said Dumbledor.
'Boo!' said Harry and Ron.
'You lost, go away!' So Lord Voldemot
disappeared.

Joshua Bobbin (8)
Innsworth Junior School, Gloucester

Strange House

Praveer crept in the house. He shouted 'Anybody home?' but nobody answered. Praveer crept one step forward. Finally a noise came from upstairs. He went upstairs but it was just a cat. So he went into his room but nobody was there. How strange.

Praveer Rai (7)

Innsworth Junior School, Gloucester

122

The Cyclops

I was on the way to the temple when suddenly
four roman guards came running by with
screaming men and women. I then ran to Ceasar
and said, 'What is the making of this?' It was the
Cyclops. I will begin a quest to kill the Cyclops.
'Come on men.'

Mitchell Hall (8)
Innsworth Junior School, Gloucester

Beccy, Chloe, Kathryn And The Pups

I came back from school to the park, my pups ran
at Beccy and she fell backwards. Kathryn and I ran
up to Beccy, she said 'Why are your pups on me?'
Then we got them off and went to the shop.

Chloe Evans (9)
Innsworth Junior School, Gloucester

The Boy Who Became Famous

This boy called Joseph was at the park with his two sisters called Fiona and Ruth and his grandad called Frank. Then a teenager who was about 15 years old broke his grandad's glasses so Joseph kicked him in the privates.

Joseph Wilson (8)
Innsworth Junior School, Gloucester

The Lost Bag

I came home without my bag. I looked for it and found it in the bathroom. My sister was taking my books out and putting them in her school bag so we could swap schools.

Caitlin Lewis (8)
Innsworth Junior School, Gloucester

Jimmy Connors

There was a boy walking up the road called Jimmy. He was running up the road and he fell over. He was sad. He had a cut on his leg. It was a deep cut. A man was running across the field. He went to help the boy.

Jimmy Connors (8)
Innsworth Junior School, Gloucester

Something I Killed

Joe crept into a cave and saw something, then
it vanished. Then a screech caught his ear. Then
something leapt out so Joe held his sword out and
killed whatever it was before he could see what
he'd killed.

Dane Smith (8)

Innsworth Junior School, Gloucester

Birthday Surprise

When I got home from school, the lights went off. I could not see anything. I was terrified. Slowly I felt my way upstairs. I barged through my bedroom door. Then the light went on again. 'You remembered my birthday. Yah!'

Beccy Frost (8)
Innsworth Junior School, Gloucester

Surprise

I came home from school and saw a note on the
stairs. It said, 'Come to the garden.'
So I did. There was a cage with a puppy in. it was
black. 'A puppy, I've always wanted a puppy!'
My heart rose higher than my head.
'Surprise!' said my mum.

Kathryn Duffy (9)
Innsworth Junior School, Gloucester

130

The Book That Spoke

My name's Beccy and yesterday I was at the
library. When I was in the children's section
someone spoke to me but it wasn't a person
who spoke to me, it was a book. All he said was
'Hello.' So with my book I ran all the way home.

Chelsea Morecroft (8)
Innsworth Junior School, Gloucester

Snowing

Rachel woke up amazed 'It's snowing!' She ran
to her drawers, pulled out her clothes, zoomed
downstairs, put her things on and went outside to
play with her friends. They made snowmen and
had snowball fights.

Mia Shilton (8)
Innsworth Junior School, Gloucester

A Sunny Day

It was Monday and my friend Kirsty and me went
to the park. We played on the swings and the
slide. Next we had an ice cream, then went home
and played. 'I'm tired, good night.' Said Kirsty and
in the morning they went to the zoo.

Izabelle Marshall (7)

Innsworth Junior School, Gloucester

Sleepover

Beccy met her friend at the park and she asked her, 'Would you like to come to a sleepover? We could have a midnight feast and watch TV.' But Izzy said that she could not come tonight. Beccy said, 'I'll try tomorrow.'

Liberty Wyatt (9)
Innsworth Junior School, Gloucester

134

Midnight!

As Sam walked home from school, she ran past
Becca's house. She went into the park then found
a little dog sitting by a tree. 'Hello chap, what's
your name?' she looked at her collar 'Midnight,
lovely name!' she picked her up, walked home
slowly and opened the door and…

Lauren Brobyn (9)
Innsworth Junior School, Gloucester

The Bell That Saved Her

Causiously I froze, my heart loudly thumping.
Fears blurred my confused mind. How did I get
trapped in this crammed photo copying room? A
terrified lady suddenly had a spectacular thought.
'I will ring the fire bell!' the second she did, the
head teacher rushed in.
'Lucy?' she gasped.

Zoe Braznell (10)
Innsworth Junior School, Gloucester

Fire!

The smoke filled my nostrils as I ran into the house that was aflame. The red flames taunted me as the black air stung my eyes. Suddenly the darkness turned to light, for it was only a dream.

Scott Harwood (11)

Innsworth Junior School, Gloucester

Ali

When Ali came home from school, there was no one to be seen. Then suddenly, as he stepped forward some more, the door opened and started to creak. The creaking got louder and louder. When he got closer to the door it got louder and louder.

Ryan Charman (10)
Innsworth Junior School, Gloucester

Red Eyes

Rebecka entered her normal gym. It was dark and grim. Suddenly a pair of red eyes glared at her through the window. Her mouth was open to scream but nothing came out.

'Cut, cut, that was horrible!' someone said. The camera stopped filming.

'You look great, but you can't act!'

Rebecka Wade-Savage (11)
Innsworth Junior School, Gloucester

Bloody Fingers

Once there was a girl called Sam whose parents were out of town. When she was looking out the window a surprised man watched her. Suddenly he knocked down the door and said, 'I am the man with bloody fingers.'

'No.'

'Yes, can I borrow some soap?' he asked.

Lewis (9)

Innsworth Junior School, Gloucester

Dark Side

Darth Vader was in a dark room. Where was everyone? It was his birthday and he had invited Stormtroopers and hired a clown. There was light coming from the kitchen. He was about to grab the door knob but then… *Boom! Boom!*
'Surprise!'
'Wow! Yum, cake!' What a birthday party.

Samuel Moylan (10)
Innsworth Junior School, Gloucester

One Stormy Night

One dark, stormy night, I heard a noise it was coming from downstairs, so I got out of my bed to see what it was. I crept downstairs to see what it was. It was really dark, I opened my living room door, it was Mum. 'Silly old me.'

Tyler Barwell (9)

Innsworth Junior School, Gloucester

142

Untitled

I was walking in the park in the middle of the
month of May. It was dark but the creaking noise
of the bushes made it sound incredibly creepy.
Suddenly there was this strange wolf. The eyes
were red as blood.
It bit me and left then I woke up.

Phil Sutton (10)
Innsworth Junior School, Gloucester

Little Brother

Quietly, the shadow stepped into my wardrobe.
That night I was terrified. In my toy box under my
bed, the light flickered. The TV flashed on 'Argh!
My eyes! Oh, it's you! Get out of my bedroom!'
my annoying, stupid dumb, little brother.
'Mum! Dad! He's in my room again!'

Tom Frost (10)
Innsworth Junior School, Gloucester

Alone

I was alone, waiting for my parents to come home. I heard a ticking noise occurring from upstairs. I thought it was a bomb! I walked upstairs. I was terrified. What was it? I arrived at the top of the stairs and realised it was my echoing clock scaring me.

Erin Buchanan (10)

Innsworth Junior School, Gloucester

145

Nightmares

The old abandoned house swayed in the wind. All
of a sudden children walked out like an invasion of
aliens. They crowded around me and murmured
'Don't you dare run.' Then I woke up everyone
else was asleep. I'd had a nightmare.

Molly Knight (10)
Innsworth Junior School, Gloucester

146

One Dark Stormy Night

One dark, stormy night the door flew open. Next the stairs creaked one by one. My heartbeat went faster. I turned the light on then it went off. What was happening? Then I turned it on again, silly me it was my mum coming to give a kiss goodnight.

Ellie Straughan (11)
Innsworth Junior School, Gloucester

What Are Hoodies Hiding?

Panting I raced home from the park. The Hoodies
were back. They always made fun of me because
of my freckles and colourful clothes. They said
they would beat me up if they saw me again.
Suddenly the wind blew, one hood fell down. Oh
gosh! Look at that wart.

Anna Duffy (11)
Innsworth Junior School, Gloucester

Oh Bob!

Shivering, I tiptoed up the stairs towards the bathroom. Something was there, hiding. Waiting to pounce, breathing heavily. I turned the handle of the door… *Phew!* What a relief! It was only my little brother, Bob! Smiling, I hugged my poor little brother. I thought he was a terrifying monster!

Rebecca Curtis (10)
Innsworth Junior School, Gloucester

Where's Mum?

Creak, the door was ajar. The wind howled outside in the dark, gloomy night. Hannah felt very sick. She was starving. Her Mum wasn't home, it was past midnight. Suddenly a huge bang came from upstairs. Hannah jumped. Bravely, she crept out of the room. Her mum had come home.

Cerys McConnochie (10)
Innsworth Junior School, Gloucester

Cinderella

Once there lived a girl called Cinderella. She lived
in a mansion with her stepmother and stepsisters;
they were very cruel and she always had to
do the work that her sisters said. There was a
dastardly cat named Louisfa who was very cruel.
Cinderella ran away from home.

Rebecca Grout (9)
Innsworth Junior School, Gloucester

The Run Away

Ron, Hermoine and Harry went to the old park.
They met Malfoy and Brandon. Lord Voldermort
came he turned all the plants into us. Then
Dumbledor came to the rescue - he put a shield
around us, but it didn't go over Harry. Let's run to
the school.

Brandon Wright (9)
Innsworth Junior School, Gloucester

152

Harry And The Stone

'Harry!' screamed Ron, the fake stone was right in front of the mirror but Harry had the real one in his pocket.

Sasha Jackson (7)
Innsworth Junior School, Gloucester

The Surfer Man!

Once upon a time there was a man who went
surfing. He fell off his surfboard but an octopus
saved him. He landed on a beach. He was safe. A
crab chopped his big toe off.

Sasha O'Brien (7)
Innsworth Junior School, Gloucester

154

The Surfer Dude

Once upon a time a man went surfing. He fell off his surfboard. Then a giant octopus threw him out of the water. He thought he was safe; then a crab came and chopped his toe off.

Owen McElvanney (8)
Innsworth Junior School, Gloucester

Ice Road Truckers

Once upon a time there was a lorry which was long. It was so long it could carry anything and it could drive on ice.

Harry Simpson (7)
Innsworth Junior School, Gloucester

Untitled

I sent roses to you to smell and painted a picture
to see but you didn't smell my roses and you
didn't see my picture. You didn't touch my hair.
You get out of here.

Liam Price (11)

Innsworth Junior School, Gloucester

Savannah The Most Beautiful Lion Ever

Savannah was the most beautiful lion in Africa.
She called all the lions to a meeting. 'Every lion be
kind and care for each other!' Savannah ordered
turning around to see the cowering pride of lions.
Now everybody would be safe in the Savannah
life, thanks to the wonderful Savannah.

Phoebe Potts (9)
Innsworth Junior School, Gloucester

Beth's Surprise

Would she be allowed or wouldn't she? Beth was hoping she'd be able to keep a Collie pup but the vet hadn't decided. The vet trotted in holding the puppy. The little dog yapped excitedly when he saw Beth.

'He's yours.' The vet smiled.

'Yes, thank you!' Beth exclaimed, delighted.

Rosie Forbes (9)

Innsworth Junior School, Gloucester

159

Seeker

I'm running, need to hide. I can hear them, their footsteps. What shall I do? Where shall I go? I can feel my heart beating. There's a ditch over there! Maybe I could hide! They're getting closer. Oh no! They've found me. Now I'm the seeker, I'm coming …

Amy Newman (9)
Innsworth Junior School, Gloucester

Mr Contrary And His Brother Mr Sensible

Mr Contrary was contrary, his brother, Mr
Sensible, was sensible. Mr Contrary woke up
with his feet where his head should have been.
But Mr Sensible woke up with his feet in the right
place. Mr Contrary put milk on his toast whilst Mr
Sensible put milk on his cornflakes.

Katie Forbes (9)
Innsworth Junior School, Gloucester

Master Killer

Master Killer was a zombie killer. One stormy night he climbed to the top of the tower in his valley where the most evil zombie lived. Killer armed his pistol and shot the zombie through the heart. The zombie turned into gold and silver dust and evaporated.

Dominic Surtees (9)
Innsworth Junior School, Gloucester

Mr Bones

Mr Bones was waiting and waiting till time has
come. Then he saw another person so off he
went to meet her on the beach.
'How are you?' said Mr Bones.
'Fine,' Replied Miss Jake.
'Do you want a drink?' asked Mr Bones.
'I love you!' said Mr Bones.

Callum McDowell (10)
Innsworth Junior School, Gloucester

Mr Strong

One day Mr Strong was walking down the street. He needed to find a job. So what he did was look in the newspaper but because he was so strong he ripped the newspaper up. He was so furious that he could not find a job in the newspaper.

Jade Honeywell (10)
Innsworth Junior School, Gloucester

My Cousin's Funeral

Bad problem, there was a strange man, Cousin.
Bang! Cousin had accidentally taken too many
pills so he blew up. There was a funeral and the
problem was that nobody came. There were
lots of empty seats but there was a rattle. Arms
appeared, he had turned into a zombie.

Harry Smith
Innsworth Junior School, Gloucester

How Armidia Healed Her Heart

All her life Armidia had felt like there was a hole in her heart - like it would never heal, but the moment she heard about the people in Transylvania and realised how much they'd lost and how much she still had, the hole was filled and she was happy.

Jasmine Manders (10)
Puller Memorial CEVA Primary School, Ware

The Boy

There once was a little boy who had been
stranded on a remote island since he was three.
He had been able to live for five years so far. He
heard a rustling in the bushes and a beastly growl,
so he grabbed his bow and arrow and he ran.

Catie Appleton (10)
Puller Memorial CEVA Primary School, Ware

The Mission Of Naymor's Life

Suddenly Naymor saw Pythagoros, the hideous beast, charge towards him but Naymor sprang from the ground and stabbed him in the head. Anxiously he turned round and spied a faded shape of Athena in a cloud. She told him to run back to his ship before the mighty storm hit.

Ashton Smith (10)

Puller Memorial CEVA Primary School, Ware

168

The Gory Battle

A trained Spartan assassin lived on an island with a zombie. He set out to kill him.
Assassin had looked all over the island when suddenly it jumped out, he stuck his sword into the zombie's body; it fell to the ground. Assassin had won the hardest battle.

Harry George (10)
Puller Memorial CEVA Primary School, Ware

Negema And The Horrible Monster

Negema was travelling to the king's palace; she'd
set off for the journey to save the king's daughter.
They went to the island of the monster called Bull
Duck Horse. They killed him and got the princess
back to the king. Negema married the king's son
and they lived happily.

Nina Jones (11)

Puller Memorial CEVA Primary School, Ware

The Brave Warrior

Suddenly a huge sea creature rose out of the roaring, blue sea. A brave young warrior was waiting; the warrior took an accurate target on the creature's head. The creature was dead at last. The brave warrior rowed home with the stolen treasure boxes taken from the sea creature's cave.

Rosalind Yates Palmer (10)
Puller Memorial CEVA Primary School, Ware

Maximus And His Final Challenge

Maximus the gladiator slowly walked out of the chamber, a spear in one hand and a shield in the other. Today he was up against an Espanola. Maximus began striking against the Spanish shield, which his opponent was holding. Maximus attacked with a jab to the heart. *Free at last!*

Kai Bryant (11)

Puller Memorial CEVA Primary School, Ware

172

Sky And The Huge Monster

Sky saw the enormous monster and she was horrified by his ugliness. She needed to kill him before he hurt any more people so she got out all her weapons and went to kill him. She got there and she shot him. He fell straight to the ground and died.

Sophi-Anne Trupia (10)
Puller Memorial CEVA Primary School, Ware

The Jogging Sprinter!

Sweat was dripping from his head, then the gun snapped. Usain sprinted as fast as he could using all the steam he had, but what's this? He was jogging to the line. It was amazing; he finished first, let alone set a new world record. It was a true miracle!

Axel Metz (11)

Puller Memorial CEVA Primary School, Ware

Medea's Quest

Fearlessly Medea accepted the challenge; the
ship set sail slowly. Athena gave Medea magical
weapons to kill Chef Cheval. Quickly Medea got
to the island and found Chef's hideout. Swiftly
Medea reflected Chef's lasers with a bronze
shield, killing Chef instantly. Medea was safe and
Chef Cheval was long gone.

Isabelle Hine (10)
Puller Memorial CEVA Primary School, Ware

The Mystery Of The Pyramids

In ancient Egypt the sun was gazing; I decided
to go inside the pyramid. The blood from my
wound was dripping; there was a flash of lightning
and Slayer appeared. I flung my sword at him he
suffered a painful death. Everybody honoured me
and I became king of Egypt.

Ellie Sutton (11)

Puller Memorial CEVA Primary School, Ware

176

Alexandra's Mission

Fearlessly Alexandra stepped foot in front of
Octoman. He was half man, half octopus. He
had wriggly, squirmy legs with a spotty, angry
human head. Alexandra held her sword in front of
Octoman, and with the Purbird's help, Octoman
was finally slain. Alexandra's happy, pretty island
was safe at last.

Lauren Elliott (10)
Puller Memorial CEVA Primary School, Ware

Bye-Bye Mr Delarose

One day a cunning assassin was set the challenge
to find and kill Rashmini Delarose. He was sniping
from a nearby window close to the victim. His
Barrett 50 Cal ready to pierce the victim. With his
Barrett 50 Cal ready, he pulled the trigger - it was
lights out for Mr Delarose.

Callum Saban (11)
Puller Memorial CEVA Primary School, Ware

178

The Scuttle Story

Unfortunately Perseus had to walk to the end
of the Earth to collect the scuttle to claim his
mother from the king who had imprisoned her.
Unfortunately Perseus had fainted and so Hades
sent Pegasus down to carry him to safety where
he healed on hopefully safe, safe land.

Elena Ray (9)
Puller Memorial CEVA Primary School, Ware

Untitled

The myth is loose. The myth is running wild in the forest and the beast sees the hero. The beast starts chasing the hero, the hero starts to stab the beast. He then dives and tries to kill the monster. The monster dies at last.

Liam Williams (10)
Puller Memorial CEVA Primary School, Ware

Cowboy Joe

One sunny day a cowboy was riding through town with his horse and a rope, he was going to fight Chimara when he came across the monster. He had a battle with the beast and fought him off. He rode back home and he was rewarded with a mighty stallion.

Harrison Rookard (9)

Puller Memorial CEVA Primary School, Ware

The Holiday

'Yes, it's my birthday,' yelled Lucy.
'Lucy, pack your bags!' shouted Mum.
'Why?' she replied.
'We are going to Ireland.'
Two hours later … they caught the plane.
In Ireland they built tents. Lucy came back and
said, 'Guys, where are you?'
'Surprise, happy birthday!'

Charlotte Barnett (10)
Roke Primary School, Kenley

The Magical Pencil Case

James looked at the pencil case, he focused on
it so hard that suddenly he went into it. James
had to tackle the pencils and the gigantic rubber.
Finally he got out but he never could become big
again.

Freddie Hawkins (10)
Roke Primary School, Kenley

Necklace

CJ was a young girl. She had a dangling red apple
necklace. In the middle of the night she awoke
still wearing the necklace.
Boom!
'Argh!' she screamed. CJ was suddenly in the
middle of nowhere. Had the necklace taken her
there?

Nina Andrew-Beddall (9)
Roke Primary School, Kenley

A Day In The Life Of The Dead

Bang! Jimmy was shot dead by a gangster called Freddie (who is very useful with a gun). Then a flash came from Jimmy's body. It was a spirit. He haunted the gangster who'd shot him for 13 days and nights. Another flash appeared. Jimmy went to Heaven.

Molly Grace (10)
Roke Primary School, Kenley

Ghost House

One day a girl called Becca visited a spooky house. She went home and told her mum who said, 'Stay away.' She ignored her mum and went back to the house.

'Argh!' she screamed. She saw five ghosts and shot out the house to her safe bed.

Skye-Louise Walker (9)

Roke Primary School, Kenley

Owl!

There was a boy who was walking through the woods. The boy saw an owl then he said, 'I hate owls, they're so stupid.' Then when he was walking he realised he was getting smaller. 'What? Help!' Then he grew wings; he saw his reflection and he was an owl.

Durrell McLean (10)
Roke Primary School, Kenley

The Story Of A Toadstool Temple

A girl finds a toadstool with a door under it but it's too small. Somehow she shrinks and goes into it. There is a brick wall so she walks out and grows again. Seconds later she finds a small man with a remote control …

Sam Pollington (10)
Roke Primary School, Kenley

The Midnight Fright

It was near midnight on Halloween. Olivia was just getting to sleep when the doorbell rang - *ding-dong!* 'Not again!' she moaned. She went downstairs to open the door. 'Nice costume,' said Olivia.
'What costume?' cackled the trick or treater. 'You can't fool me … wait … Jake … where's your head?'

Loveday Lawton (10)
Roke Primary School, Kenley

189

Ghost Cemetery!

An old grave rocked back and forth at the
cemetery. Spookily a ghost appeared from the
tombstone. But people didn't believe it was real.
The ghost appeared and Tom and Sarah were
there. He killed them both in return for them
killing him. A ghost cursed him!

Oliver Fielding (10)
Roke Primary School, Kenley

190

Dead

Tom and his dad went to the gloomy cemetery to put roses on his mum's grave. Suddenly his dad dropped down dead. 'What shall I do?' screamed Tom.

Minutes later Tom heard a groaning noise. 'Oooah! His dad was walking towards him with outstretched arms. 'Only joking,' laughed his dad.

Ryan Allalat (9)
Roke Primary School, Kenley

Ghostbusters 3

In New York there was a marshmallow stand near
the building where the marshmallow man got
melted, but then the marshmallow stand tipped
over from the blowing wind. It went into the
marshmallow man then it grew soft and tall, then
the ghostbusters came.

Charlie Coleman (10)
Roke Primary School, Kenley

Pixie Life

Elle the Pixie called her friends because she heard something. They saw a magical path - bright and colourful. She needed a new life and wanted to get there quickly. Her friends Nattaly and Clare came with her. The place was called Pixitopia and it sounded nice.

Ramiah Yousaf (10)
Roke Primary School, Kenley

Drag Me To Hell!

Emily and Courtney were waiting for the film
called 'Drag Me To Hell' to start.
'Finally,' sighed Courtney.
'This film is spooky,' said Emily quietly. Suddenly
a hand came out of the screen and dragged
Courtney into …*Hell!*
'Courtney!' shouted Emily.
She disappeared and was never ever seen again!

Kaylan Barzinji (10)
Roke Primary School, Kenley

194

Jordan And The Picture

Jordan is in the art gallery. She is looking at a
picture, a space picture. She stares for so long
that she faints. All of a sudden she wakes up in the
middle of nowhere; all she could see were stars.
'I am in space.'

James Penfold (10)
Roke Primary School, Kenley

Bang!

Bang! Jack fell, dead. The armed terrorist ran.
There was a blinding flash. Jack's spirit rose
steadily out of his body. *I'm dead,* he thought. 'I'm
transparent,' he muttered grumpily. 'When am I
going to Heaven?' he asked himself.
'Don't be so sure, ha, ha, ha,' exclaimed a fiery
figure …

Joseph Pett (10)
Roke Primary School, Kenley

196

Halloween!

Mary strolled to her door. Someone had knocked.
'Who could that be?'
A man was ready to strike. She saw who it was.
She called the police. He went to jail.

Morgan Wilkins-Oliver (10)
Roke Primary School, Kenley

Aliens!

Years ago aliens appeared, scaring people because
they wanted a McDonald's Happy Meal.
'£100,' said the staff member to the alien.
'*What*?' said the alien in shock. 'That's a rip off!'
The alien paid the money so he could have the
toy spaceship in the Happy Meal to get home
today.

Oliver Addison (9)
Roke Primary School, Kenley

On Duty

The Russians were bombing the Nazis in their war planes. The Nazis were fighting back in their war planes. It was a terrible fight but it had to be done. Then, out of nowhere, there was a Russian leader, hoping to kill the Nazis. Then he shot them. It ended.

Andrew McSorley (10)
Roke Primary School, Kenley

The Nightmare

John was in his room asleep. He was having a terrible nightmare. He was having a dream that he was in an isolated park, but he wasn't alone; there was a ghost behind him, moving like him. Suddenly it jumped on him and he woke up.

Lawrence Tooze (9)
Roke Primary School, Kenley

Tortoise And Pear

One bright day Tortoise was admiring his flowers
when suddenly Pear challenged him to a race.
Tortoise accepted the challenge and the next
day the race took place. When the ref blew his
whistle, Tortoise gobbled up Pear.
A million years later Tortoise reached the finish
line.

Joe Webster (10)
Roke Primary School, Kenley

The Rock Stars

The band was up on stage; they were very scared. Suddenly a man changed the singer and fired the other one. When the band started, the singer was amazing, everyone loved his singing. He sang for hours and hours. Everyone's favourite song was on today. Everyone loved him.

Dylan Borg Piscopo (10)
Roke Primary School, Kenley

The Dare!

Once there were four mice in a hole. They were frightened of a scary monster. The mice could not get any cheese because of that scary monster. One day a mouse said, 'I dare you to get some cheese.'
'OK.'
The mouse crept out … 'It's a sofa! Come on guys!'

Ayman Gharbaoui (10)
Roke Primary School, Kenley

Abducted

Jacob woke to a blue light shining through his window. Then suddenly he flew straight out of his window. 'Argh!' screamed Jacob. In two minutes he was inside the *alien ship!* Face to face with some slimy, green aliens. Then he heard his mum's voice.
'Get up!' Time for school.'

Luke Perrott (10)
Roke Primary School, Kenley

Disaster

Trouble-making Mildred made a potion …
Suddenly she knocked it over. 'Oh no! Tabby!'
Her cat started to lap it up … *Bang!* Tabby had
turned into a horrific griffin. Mildred said the
reverse spell and there sat Tabby as though
nothing had happened.

Abbie Perryman (10)
Roke Primary School, Kenley

The Scary Playground

One cold day Sara went to the park in the playground. She saw a gravestone with her mum and dad's names on it. She started to weep hysterically. Suddenly she heard a scary voice. 'Ha, ha, ha! You're here forever.'
'Get me out of here! It's against my human rights.'

Meera Padhiar (9)
Roke Primary School, Kenley

206

My Room Of Horror

I woke up in my room of horror. Bats circled in
the corner. The terrifying thing was I thought that
my parents had turned my room into a graveyard.
Zombies were crowding around me; my heart
was pounding. Suddenly I woke up in my proper
room. I was safe.

Charlotte Collins (9)
Roke Primary School, Kenley

207

Super Boy!

Once upon a time there was a boy called John who was very weak. One day he was in the woods when he saw an extraordinary rock, so he picked it up. It sent a radioactive wave through his body. From that day on he helped everyone he saw.

Zain Kara (10)
Roke Primary School, Kenley

All Wrong

At school the worst witch had to make a
potion that made everyone giggle. Mildred used
slimy slugs, snails and spiders' legs. When her
classmates drank the potion they turned into pigs.
They could not turn back to normal so they were
stuck like that forever.

Louise Hollands (10)
Roke Primary School, Kenley

Friendship

There were two lovely girls called Lara and
Hayley. They always messed around in the house.
The next day it was Lara's birthday so she got up
and went to Hayley's house. *Knock, knock!* 'Oh
no, she's not in. Shall I ring her? *Ring, ring*. 'Oh no!'

Lara Waters (9)
Roke Primary School, Kenley

The Whoopee Cushion

I was at a very fun party. Emma had a whoopee
cushion in her party bag, she told me to sit down
so I did and suddenly the room filled with a loud
splirt! Then I stood up and realised Emma had put
a whoopee cushion under my seat. 'Argh!'

Stella Brooke-Jones (8)

St James' Primary School, Emsworth

Monster

I've seen a lot of monsters, one liked Tottenham
Hotspurs, one was green and hairy and another
was as cute as a fairy. I liked the one with canines
because he lived in the Pennines. I also liked
the one that floated because he was chocolate-
coated. Crikey!

Niall Malik (10)
St Martin's School, London

212

Untitled

There I was, running through the meadow
desperately trying to find you. The clouds were
dark and my heart was thumping so loudly.
Suddenly I saw a silhouette. 'Who could it be?' I
said to myself.
A voice came to me, calling, 'I love you.'

Abhishek Lakhani (12)
St Martin's School, London

Over The Top

Shells from high above lurking in midair and
they drop in a split second. Death hangs in the
balance, not just from the bullet or the machine
gun as it rattles away continuously, but also the
determination to go out there and fight, fight
forever on.

Daniel Philpott (11)
St Martin's School, London

The Man Who Lived In A Tree

There was once a man who lived in a tree. He fell
off it and broke his knee. He started crying and
called for help. Since the tree was abandoned by
a motorway that was noisy, no one heard him. So
there stayed the man that fell off the tree - sad.

Akibodun Akiwumi (10)
St Martin's School, London

The Crazy House

Once there was a very alarming house. It was abandoned and then a royal family came. They were on horses. They found the house. They went inside. The door squeaked loudly. It was madness there. There was toast flying everywhere and knives trying to cut off their feet. Oh no!

Nyah Paris (7)
Shinfield St Mary's CE Junior School, Shinfield

Untitled

There was a boy called Joe and his dog called
Spike. One day they were walking in the noisy
green forest when they came to a haunted house.
It looked creepy and very old. They wanted to
look inside. Joe was scared but Spike ran straight
in so Joe followed.

Nicholas Avenell (7)

Shinfield St Mary's CE Junior School, Shinfield

The Day I Disappeared

I just came out of the shops. My mum was waiting
for me so I got in the car and I was sweating.
Then suddenly it all went pitch-black. I felt like I
was gone forever but then lights came and I saw
bloody walls and … what was that?

Morgan Chard (8)
Shinfield St Mary's CE Junior School, Shinfield

Untitled

There was a brave boy called Zon. He was climbing a huge mountain and was near the top. Suddenly he slipped and just hung on the top. Then there was a massive avalanche. He was trying to hold on to something but he couldn't find anything. He went crashing down.

Conor Clarke (8)
Shinfield St Mary's CE Junior School, Shinfield

219

The Adventure To The Museum

Me and my brother went to a museum. We saw lots of big models, some dinosaur eggs and then people went into a very huge door. Then suddenly nobody came out. We went into the door. Then it took us to a small island and we were hungry.

Callum Cox (8)
Shinfield St Mary's CE Junior School, Shinfield

220

The Witch And The Cat In The Forest

The greedy witch and cat walked to the forest to
go and get some strawberries. The strawberries
were bright red and juicy. The witch ate them
in one big bite. The witch was mean and nasty
and the cat was called Sparky. Suddenly they
disappeared into a dark hole.

Ella Cox (7)

Shinfield St Mary's CE Junior School, Shinfield

The Missing Car

One stormy night my dad broke the television so he decided to go to my nan's house. He looked for the car keys but he could not find them. He looked outside and the car was gone. Who or what could have taken his car? Maybe it was a stranger.

Lewis Dallimore (8)
Shinfield St Mary's CE Junior School, Shinfield

222

The Unknown World

Once there was an evil wizard who lived in a
skanky cell with a ninja granny. She kept the
wizard hostage. The wizard broke out. Suddenly
he ran for Earth. He jumped and landed. He
howled in pain. The granny did the same and
kicked him in the face. Ow!

Joshua East (8)
Shinfield St Mary's CE Junior School, Shinfield

223

Hayley And The Paper Aeroplane

Crackle, crackle!
'Are you okay Hayley?'
'Oh no, my paper aeroplane flew to the park.'
She burst out with tears of water. 'Will you get it?'
'Yes.'
They got it out.
'Now we can play again but first I have to paint it
pink, blue, red, orange, purple, yellow, brown.'

Morgan Gavaghan (8)
Shinfield St Mary's CE Junior School, Shinfield

Untitled

In a strange town there lived a young hero whose
name was Camboy. A nasty monster came
to town. Camboy was going to have his first
superhero adventure. He did not know it was not
training. It was really a monster. It was not what
he was expecting. 'Help! Help!'

Lucy Grant (7)
Shinfield St Mary's CE Junior School, Shinfield

Untitled

One day Hayley went to the beach with her dad,
mum and sister and brother. They had brilliant
fun. They had a picnic together then they got
their costumes on and went swimming - that
was really exciting. Then they got a drink and …
suddenly a shark was eaten by a whale.

Megan Gravestock (8)
Shinfield St Mary's CE Junior School, Shinfield

Untitled

I found a teddy with one ear. To fix her she must sit upon a magic chair. The chair was missing. I went underground. The chair was there. I had to defeat Huggles. I brought out my lion, Huggles ran. The bear sat on the chair with two ears again.

Lauren Hemmings (8)
Shinfield St Mary's CE Junior School, Shinfield

Untitled

The king was far away in a magical kingdom. He lived in an enormous castle. One day he saw a pirate ship and he was very worried. The pirates were coming to the castle. The king shouted to the guards, 'Quick, lock the doors!' But then suddenly the pirates appeared …

Joshua Jackman (7)
Shinfield St Mary's CE Junior School, Shinfield

Untitled

A boy called Ben went to a forest with a dog called Max. Ben got bitten by a poisonous mosquito. A huge bear appeared from behind the big rocks. Ben was scared. Max started to bark and growl at the bear. The bear ran off. Max had saved Ben's life.

Trey Mattingley (7)
Shinfield St Mary's CE Junior School, Shinfield

Museum Night

Me and my brother were at a museum. We saw a
door. It said on a piece of paper 'Do Not Open'.
We opened it. We were in Henry VIII's castle.
We ran to the door, it was not there. Henry was
coming. Me and my brother were very scared.

Matthew McDermott (7)
Shinfield St Mary's CE Junior School, Shinfield

Mission Impossible

Hi, my name is Ethan and I am underground
where it stinks. My friend Boldy is on top of me
and I need to get to him before the nasty killer
gets here or the mission will have failed. Who
knows what that nasty killer will do to me …

Anton Miller (7)
Shinfield St Mary's CE Junior School, Shinfield

The Haunted House

The gloomy haunted house was so smoky that a ghost could pop out in front of you and scare you out of the house. But Sparky the cat wasn't scared of anything. Suddenly a massive dinosaur appeared from the shadows and frightened Sparky the cat away. Sparky never came back.

Trinity Norris (7)
Shinfield St Mary's CE Junior School, Shinfield

Untitled

Once upon a time there was a boy called Bill. Bill was cool because he had a super dog. The dog's name was zapper. Later they would have a big mission to do. One day there was a big famine. Curiously they ran. Zapper jumped and zapped the snakes.

Jason Scott (8)
Shinfield St Mary's CE Junior School, Shinfield

The Mystery Of The Lost Diamonds

There once was an unusual land. Linda, Ashley
and James walked down the hill and found a
chest. It was open. James looked in and thought
he saw a gleaming, silver, shiny ... nothing! But
there was a map in the chest. Was it a map to find
the lost diamonds?

Louisa Taylor (7)
Shinfield St Mary's CE Junior School, Shinfield

234

Oggy And The Enormous Boom

One day Oggy went to a shop. Suddenly he felt
an enormous boom! It shook the concrete. Then
Oggy followed the enormous boom. When he
got to the enormous boom Oggy was very, very
terrified of a gigantic volcano. He slowly climbed
and suddenly he was on top. Oggy slipped.

Harry Willoughby (8)
Shinfield St Mary's CE Junior School, Shinfield

Spooked ...

I creaked open the door and peeked inside.
Something or someone was there. Cautiously
I crept in. 'Hello,' I whispered. No answer.
Suddenly the door slammed behind me. I spun
round, it wasn't there now. A light flickered on
and off behind me. I turned around slowly, there
it was!

Natalie Scott (10)
Shinfield St Mary's CE Junior School, Shinfield

Untitled

One day in an abandoned street two sides met.
They hid in the broken building.
Bang! There went the rifle, both teams jumped
out. 'War!' they all shouted. Shotguns shooting,
nunchucks flying, swinging around poles, waiting
behind bins. Finally three versus three. One ninja
did a spinning kick … Who won?

Luke White (10)
Shinfield St Mary's CE Junior School, Shinfield

When It Attacked!

As Jamie slowly approached he saw the sign. It said 'No Entry'. *I must retrieve it,* thought Jamie. *I swore on it.* He entered and saw a stone. 'There it is.' He grabbed.

'Argh!' screamed someone. Jamie started to run out of the cave. It appeared at the creaky door.

Oliver East (10)
Shinfield St Mary's CE Junior School, Shinfield

Mystery

I was in my classroom and the time froze. I saw
people running then I saw ghosts drifting away.
Then I saw my grandmother. She spoke to me.
She dropped to the floor then I heard chains. I
heard hooves, where was I? I don't know. Help!
Then it started.

Georgia Moreby (10)
Shinfield St Mary's CE Junior School, Shinfield

The Haunted House

One dark, cold night lights started to flicker in the old haunted house which stood by the green swamp. A figure walked by the window. He looked like my school teacher. 'Why was he there?' I asked myself. Suddenly I dropped my bags and ran inside to help him, but …

Josh Knight (10)
Shinfield St Mary's CE Junior School, Shinfield

Bloodstained Windows

I slammed open the moss covered door. The old church was demolished. The stained glass windows were dripping with blood. I was the only living thing there. I quickly shivered; it felt as if someone had walked over my grave. The brown, creaky eagle's eyes stood staring down at me.

Maddison Hodder (11)

Shinfield St Mary's CE Junior School, Shinfield

The Spooky Lake

The thirteen-year-old girl went to the creepy lake at the break of dawn. She was on her own. She noticed there was a bubbling, mystery thing in the water. The thing was getting closer, the bubbles were turning green. After that mysterious day she was never seen again.

Charlie Cox (11)
Shinfield St Mary's CE Junior School, Shinfield

Under My Bed

I curled up in my bed. I heard a creepy noise.
I wondered where it was coming from. I was
frightened so I stomped to the cracked door but
it was locked. I kept hearing noises under my bed.
I stood and bent down and looked under. 'Argh!
Help me!'

Kelsey Sims (10)
Shinfield St Mary's CE Junior School, Shinfield

The Dark Subway

I walked into the subway, looked left then right.
Ghost-like voices came from either end. I stood
there waiting, waiting. Only me and a crooked
man stood by the demolished subway. I had
nothing for comfort, the lights flickered in horror.
Argh! I fell down deep. The man cackled.

Molly O'Brien (10)
Shinfield St Mary's CE Junior School, Shinfield

Mystery Alley

One dark night I was walking home by myself, as I thought I would take a shortcut but I didn't really know where I was going. But then I came to a darkened alley. I heard a scream. Then I woke up in a hospital, with broken legs and arms.

Mia Walton (10)

Shinfield St Mary's CE Junior School, Shinfield

The Scrapyard

The lines of dead and derelict trains are said to be haunted by the ghosts of the people who made them. One night, only two years ago, it happened. I was in the scrapyard when a ghostly voice shouted, 'Do not come any further into my realm.' Suddenly, *bang!*

Owen Mace (10)
Shinfield St Mary's CE Junior School, Shinfield

The Giant Pinball Machine

The stupid boy ran into an abandoned arcade
then plugged in the pinball machine and started
playing it. All of a sudden the boy was zapped
into the pinball game inside a transparent ball.
Someone must have yanked the spring which
launched him roughly into the pinball game's
playing field.

Bradley Browne (11)

Shinfield St Mary's CE Junior School, Shinfield

247

What Was In The Cupboard?

It was a cold, dark night. I was in bed when suddenly the lights went out. A power cut! I heard footsteps, creeping up the stairs. A crash of thunder struck. The door slammed open. The cupboard shook. I moved slowly towards it. I woke up in hospital. What happened?

Ben Green (10)
Shinfield St Mary's CE Junior School, Shinfield

Caribbean Carnival

I was at a Caribbean carnival with loads of other people. We were dancing and being jolly, wearing fantastic hats, moving along with the crowd. There were throngs of people dressed in colourful costumes, laughing and singing. Although the music was banging heavily through my head, I still enjoyed it.

Tia Drinkwater (10)
Shinfield St Mary's CE Junior School, Shinfield

My Sister's Strangler

I was at home watching television with my sister and suddenly all of the lights went off and then they turned on unexpectedly. My sister was gone. I looked for her everywhere but she was nowhere to be seen. I saw a man outside holding my sister by the neck …

Afiya Vanden Bossche (10)
Shinfield St Mary's CE Junior School, Shinfield

Dark Alley

It was a late Friday night, I was walking to my friend's house. I began to take a shortcut through an alley. It was quiet. I knew something was wrong. I knew I was being watched, so I walked faster. I listened. I could hear footsteps coming closer behind me …

Hannah Grover (11)
Shinfield St Mary's CE Junior School, Shinfield

Gone!

I was at the amusement park about to go on a ride with my friend. Then all of a sudden she was gone. I started to panic and looked frantically around the park. Then I saw her on a ride with a man. She was screaming. He had a gun.

Jordani Lynch (10)
Shinfield St Mary's CE Junior School, Shinfield

The Dark Blood

I was strolling back from a late night party. I walked down the steps and into the subway. As I was walking, I saw drops of blood on the floor. I walked further. I saw a knife. I walked further and saw a body dripping with dark blood. I screamed.

Eva Malin (10)

Shinfield St Mary's CE Junior School, Shinfield

The Shadow

I was alone, watching the red sun set around me, leaving the wind to brush my face. I suddenly saw a dark figure moving slowly in the bushes. Then it disappeared. I leaned over the edge of the waterfall, then all I remember was that I was falling down, down …

Anna Watts (11)
Shinfield St Mary's CE Junior School, Shinfield

The Haunted House

One miserable, rainy Sunday night Mark walked
quickly to his house when he noticed that the
windows were smashed. Suddenly he could hear
a scream coming from inside. He crept through
the door in fear. He woke up the next morning in
a field with blood pouring from his head.

Liam Tindell (11)
Shinfield St Mary's CE Junior School, Shinfield

The Crater

A man stood at the edge of the crater, staring into it. He heard a roar. He saw an evil red and yellow tooth. He woke up at the bottom of the crater. He was lying in his own blood. He saw a pair of red eyes staring at him.

Scott Winton (11)
Shinfield St Mary's CE Junior School, Shinfield

Max And Lila

There once was a giant called Max. One day
a man told him there was a giant called Lila in
the black castle. Max smashed the doors of the
castle. He stumbled up the stairs. Max saw a key.
He grabbed it and opened the cage and they ran
away.

Matilda Lahiff (10)
Streatham & Clapham High School, London

The Tiger

This tiger was dying. I knew it was. There was a withering look in its eyes. It was the last tiger on Earth. I walked cautiously towards the cage and unlocked the bolt. The tiger's eyes glistened and it bowed its head. I knew then it was truly saying thanks.

Katherine Rix (10)
The Pointer School, Blackheath

258

One Trick Beats Another Trick

Jimmy, a beetle, lived with his mama. One day Evil
the lizard pattered up to trick him. 'Little beetle,
what'd you most desire to eat?' But Jimmy knew
this trick.
'Lavender soup with gravel grindings,' he replied.
'And right now my mama is cooking some!' Jimmy
chuckled and he left.

Esther Doel (9)
The Pointer School, Blackheath

259

Tom's Secret

As I walked down the stairs, I heard a noise. It was a letter for me. It said, 'Dear Tom, you have a secret adventure to go on. On your way, you have to find three magic rocks and they are red, blue and yellow. Good luck. From Mr Magic'.

Shaan Sandhu (9)
The Pointer School, Blackheath

Trickery

I was alone in a dark room. I was terrified. I saw
the eyes of a man looking at me sternly, but then
I turned the lights on and the eyes disappeared.
How strange, I thought, *I will sleep with the light on
from now on.*

Seb Lloyd (9)
The Pointer School, Blackheath

Cliff Hanger

I was hanging on a cliff. The cliff edge was
cracking. One hand slipped, I grabbed for my
phone and rang the fire brigade. They were
coming. Then my other hand slipped. I fell - only
just able to grab another ledge. Would they make
it in time?

Hudson Farley-Moore (10)
The Pointer School, Blackheath

The New Family Member

I raced home, my heart beating fiercely. Mum told me I'd have a surprise. I pushed the door and to my surprise, I saw a little girl waving at me. 'This is your new sister,' Mum said, beaming with excitement. My heart dropped. I was no longer number one.

Saraya Joseph (10)
The Pointer School, Blackheath

The Dragon

Dragons aren't real, right? Wrong! The komodo dragon has been discovered and I discovered a flying one. I doubt my friends or anyone else will believe me. But one day they will, when they see the evidence, then they'll wish they'd believed me.

Harrison Marsh (9)
The Pointer School, Blackheath

The Spy Game Strikes

As I strode down the hallway, I got out my dart gun, ready to obliviate the enemy, when my mum told me to have my dinner and to stop playing with that horrible thing. I told her that it was contradictory to say that, because she bought it for me.

Edward McAllister (8)
The Pointer School, Blackheath

The Puppy

'It's my birthday,' cried Tom as he ran down the stairs. In the kitchen, he saw a box with breathing holes. When his mum opened the box, a horrifyingly ugly puppy jumped out. 'It's so ugly!' Tom shouted.

'He'll grow out of it,' laughed his mum.

Charlotte Parkes (10)

The Pointer School, Blackheath

Creepy Coffins

'Oh no!' shivered Kate. Kate was lost in a graveyard. Suddenly the tops of the coffins flew off. The dead bodies sat up and flew out of their coffins. Kate was surrounded by dead bodies. They got closer and closer and then no one saw Kate again.

Amber Hunt (10)
The Pointer School, Blackheath

Love Awakened
(Re-write of Sleeping Beauty)

The prince stormed into the chamber and saw a fascinating girl lying there. He kissed her passionately. The room was filled with shimmering light as three waiting fairies flashed fireworks out of their wands. They fled the tower, riding on a magical horse into the sunset, and lived happily together.

Serena Shakshir (10)

The Study Preparatory School, London

My Pony Was Not In His Field

Clasping his headcollar, I looked around and
yelled. He had disappeared. I swivelled my
disappointed eyes towards a black van. I heard
a neigh and rushed towards it. As the van
accelerated away, I hauled open the back door
and my brave pony jumped out. 'Foolish people,'
I shouted loudly.

Freya Hough (9)
The Study Preparatory School, London

The Mighty Sea Dragon

Alone on the cliff he wandered, colossal waves pounding far below, with a blood-curdling roar the sea monster leapt angrily from the waves. It reared up to full height with deafening roars. He grabbed his sword and plunged it deep within the monster's leg. Shuddering, the monster painfully died.

Amber Cater (9)

The Study Preparatory School, London

270

The Doll On Top Of The Cupboard

'Don't slam that door! Vibrations knock me off the cupboard,' declared Emma Doll.
'Oops!' apologised Megan.
'I'm thirsty,' complained Emma.
Megan left, slamming the bedroom door, and down tumbled Emma. Megan returned with some water. 'Emma, what happened?'
'All vibrations knock me over,' sniffed Emma.
'Move me to the chair.'

Navya Lobo (10)
The Study Preparatory School, London

The Rapunzel Mishap

Rapunzel, a beautiful girl, was trapped in an immense tower. Rapunzel's golden hair grew long and by climbing it you could reach her and see her concealed beauty. Once an obese prince spotted Rapunzel. 'Drop your hair,' he called. She did but he was heavy; her hair ripped off! Ouch!

Laura Dyamond (9)
The Study Preparatory School, London

Her Dog Went To The Butcher But She Fetched Him Back Forever

There was a love that couldn't be broken, not even by death. The girl and her dog trekked through terrifying storms. Finally, exhausted, they rested under a tree. Death overcame them and there they slept for the last time; but they lived on forever, in paradise. Their love never failed.

Kate Sibbald (10)
The Study Preparatory School, London

Homeward Bound, A Monster That Rose From The Sea

We heard a mighty roar! It was the dreadful sea monster, but I had a plan. Terrified, we sailed into the monster's vast mouth. We were in! Next I stabbed my magic sword deep into his deadly throat. The monster let out a deafening roar. We escaped - just in time.

Lauren Lee (9)
The Study Preparatory School, London

Not So Happily Ever After

And so it continued in Fairytale Land, Hansel
and Gretel discovered they were diabetic. The
witch ate pork and apple sauce and died. *Oops,
wrong apple!* The Mad Hatter went on to star in
Tarantino movies. And the prince continued to
chase the girls. Nothing went right. Disaster was
looming.

Isabella Forshaw (9)
The Study Preparatory School, London

275

The Three Little Piggies

Having finished building their houses, the three piggies went inside to wait for Wolf. Piggy One phoned the others. 'Where's Wolf?'
'He's got detention!' chortled Piggy Two.
Believing it was safe, they scampered outside.
Unfortunately, truant Wolf was lurking nearby and although they ran, he caught and ate all three!

Jessica Price (10)

The Study Preparatory School, London

Who's Coming To Tea?

Looking down the hole, she falls, tumbling and
twirling. 'We're late!' she hears. A strange figure,
with crazy, bright orange hair, a wicked smile, a
funny-looking hat and holding a teacup, appears.
'Is there a party going on?' she asks.
'Yes my dear, it's your brother's eighth birthday
party!'

Nicola Saclley (10)
The Study Preparatory School, London

The Journey From Captivity

Oliver awoke, not at home. Men burst in with guns. Oliver tried to escape into the forest and was lost for days. He sat down, waiting. Suddenly a woman came and took him to her hut. She fed and healed him. They walked through the forest, all the way home.

Zoe Combe (9)
The Study Preparatory School, London

Alone In A House Emma Read Her Horror Story

Emma went to sleep and dreamt about ghosts. She woke up to hear her bedside alarm clock ringing. She reached out to stop the noise when something pushed against her hand, the clock stopped ringing. Scared, she crept downstairs to find that her breakfast was already made on the table!

Clara Pohlen Schachtschabel (10)

The Study Preparatory School, London

Information

We hope you have enjoyed reading this book - and that you will continue to enjoy it in the coming years.

If you like reading and writing, drop us a line or give us a call and we'll send you a free information pack. Alternatively visit our website at www.youngwriters.co.uk

Write to:
Young Writers Information,
Remus House,
Coltsfoot Drive,
Peterborough,
PE2 9JX

Tel: (01733) 890066
Email: youngwriters@forwardpress.co.uk